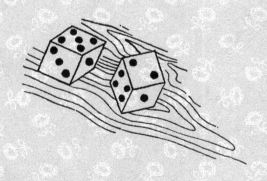

This volume is consecrated to that dramatic and highly colorful song, FRANKIE AND JOHNNY, which can claim an important place in our folk literature, in the sense that it does not owe its long life and popularity to the printed page.

Mr. Huston's adaptation of the song for the stage is based on the many versions which he has discovered throughout the country. Twenty of these versions appear at the back of the book, with a note on the St. Louis one, which which is the most authentic of them all.

There are many who can sing FRANKIE AND JOHNNY, but very few who know about its origin or have any idea of the gay opulence of the *milieu* where it came into existence. Messrs. Huston and Covarrubias have ably seen to it that those who are curious to know more can now be satisfied.

Frankie and Johnny

Frankie and Johnny

By
John Huston

Illustrated by
Miguel Covarrubias

DOVER PUBLICATIONS, INC.
Mineola, New York

Bibliographical Note

This Dover edition, first published by Dover Publications, Inc., in 2015, is an unabridged republication of the edition originally published by Albert and Charles Boni, Inc., New York, in 1930. The book is being reprinted exactly as it was published in an effort to preserve the consistency of the original edition and its historical context, which include some regrettable, potentially offensive elements.

Library of Congress Cataloging-in-Publication Data

Huston, John, 1906–1987.
    Frankie and Johnny / John Huston ; illustrated by Miguel Covarrubias.
        p. cm.
    ISBN-13: 978-0-486-79467-9
    ISBN-10: 0-486-79467-9
    I. Title.
PS3515.U83F7 2015
812'.54—dc23

                                                        2014039159

Manufactured in the United States by Courier Corporation
79467901   2015
www.doverpublications.com

FOR
DOROTHY

Contents

9

11

I am indebted to ABBE NILES, R. W. GORDON,
BILLY PIERCE, H. QUALLI CLARK,
and BEN APPLEGATE
who helped me find the
original Frankie

Frankie and Johnny

A PLAY

Cast

JOHNNY

FRANKIE

SHERIFF

NELLY BLY

LILA

THE MADAM, *Johnny's Mother*

BARTENDER

PIANO PLAYER

PRIZEFIGHTER

The girls in red, and the ten macks

15

Prologue

The curtains part to the sustained beats of a funeral march. The scene is at the scaffold, where Frankie stands with a noose around her throat. Below her are the Sheriff, the Madam, the Bartender, and a throng of harlots and loose gentlemen. They stand in various postures of grief, with averted faces and downcast eyes.

17

SHERIFF

Has the condemned anythin' to say afore we take in the slack?

FRANKIE

I know I'm bound for a better land.

SHERIFF

Aye, that ye are, Frankie,—an' we all wish ye God speed.

FRANKIE

An' I ain't afeard, not even if damnation is my lot. I know I done wrong. Ye can hoist when ye've a mind to.

19

SHERIFF

An' ye won't hold it agin us, Frankie? Not me, nowise,—it ain't my doin'.

FRANKIE

I'll breathe out a blessin' on ye, Sheriff, with my last livin' breath.

SHERIFF

Have ye no partin' wish,—no last request? What should we do with the remains?

FRANKIE

Put 'em aside his.

SHERIFF

Johnny's?

FRANKIE

Aye, Johnny's.

SHERIFF

There's where ye'll rest, I swear it, Frankie.

20

FRANKIE

God bless ye, Sheriff. There, six foot down aside him, I may find peace.

SHERIFF

An' he can't be askin' nothin' of ye.

FRANKIE

But if he did, Sheriff, he could have what he wanted.

SHERIFF

Aye, I know. Ye'd give him all he'd take.....But have ye no bequest, no testament to make?

FRANKIE

If it's worldly goods ye mean, I have naught. I gave him all I had.

SHERIFF

Johnny?

FRANKIE

Aye, Johnny. But I have a testament, leastwise a testamonial. An' I do bequeathe it to them as might need it.

SHERIFF

An' what might it be, Frankie? Ye'd best hasten as the time is gettin' shorter.

FRANKIE

I will the memory a me to them as it'll stand in hand.

SHERIFF

An' who are they?

FRANKIE

Whoever shall be born to love. Let them hear my tale,—how I loved an' done wrong.

CROWD

Aye, Frankie, that we will. Ye can bank on it, Frankie, we'll tell your story.

22

FRANKIE

Tell oney what happened,—what you yourselves saw. Keep it straight. Mind ye don't add nothin'.

SHERIFF

It can stand as it is. It don't need no trimmin'.

FRANKIE

I bequeathes my story to them as may need it, to maidens an' youths who will love an' know heartache. Let them hear my tale how I loved an' done wrong. So— "When the Sheriff cuts the slender cord, An' my soul goes up to meet the Lord, Say not I died in vain."
The dismal cadence of the funeral march is distorted into the Frankie and Johnny tune. The volume of the music increases as the lights dim out.

Scene One

A barroom. Lila, a drunken chippy, and the Prizefighter are dancing. Johnny, the Madam, Nelly Bly, and the Piano Player look on. The Bartender is stacking glasses.

25

LILA

Dance me easy, Prizefighter. Don't wrassle me so, or I may slop over on ye.

MADAM

Now, Lila, do like the gent wants. Be merry, dearie.
to Prizefighter
Her tongue's a mite sharp, but she don't mean ye no harm.

LILA

Whoops,—ki-yi! The tide's a-risin'!
She falls. The Madam helps her to a chair.

27

MADAM

Do ye want a good smacking?
to the others
Her stummick's upset, pore child.

LILA

shrieking
I got 'em. They're a-climbin' up under my dresses.

PRIZEFIGHTER

to the Bartender
Squirrel.

BARTENDER

A peg.

LILA

They're in under my skirts.

MADAM

slapping Lila's ears
It'll clear her head.

28

PRIZEFIGHTER

to Bartender
The same.

BARTENDER

It ain't covered.

PRIZEFIGHTER

I laid down a dime.

BARTENDER

Put up your nickel or it's back in the vat.
Bartender and Prizefighter both grab for the glass. The Prizefighter seizes it from the Bartender who reaches for his mallet and brings it down on the Prizefighter's head. The Prizefighter sags to his knees.
The rat's swallered the glass.
Johnny goes to the bar, puts his arm around the Prizefighter and hoists him straight. Then, sliding his hand into the Prizefighter's pocket, he brings out some coins.

29

JOHNNY

His speech is impeded by his hare lip.
to the unconscious Prizefighter, conversationally
Why yes, I will. That's more'n kind. What?—
ain't that a little costly? But just as ye says.
to the Bartender
We're to have the best the house can offer. An' you
can keep the change.
Johnny drains his own and the Prizefighter's glass.
to the Prizefighter
What? What was that? He's a-puttin' suthin' over
on us, ye says? Well, Mr. Barkeep, we'll stand none
a that. We ain't buyin' hog wash.
The Prizefighter shows signs of reviving. Johnny
nails him with his right and resumes his load. He
drinks again.
to the Bartender
He says that is more like it, an' would ye please set
out the bottle.
Johnny puts the bottle first to the Prizefighter's
lips, then to his own.
Nelly Bly sidles to the bar.
30

NELLY

Ye looks beautiful in yer new suit, Johnny.

JOHNNY

discarding his victim

Well, I got the form for it. Wet yer whistle.

NELLY

They tells how Frankie paid one hunnerd dollars for it. You look wunnerful in it. Ye shows it off so good.

JOHNNY

I'd a-rather she'd a-given me the cash.

NELLY

I thought at the time I bet he'd rather had the coin. I says it was downright selfish a-dressin' him up 'cause she took pleasure lookin' at him an' him in need a the dough.

JOHNNY

Aye, I had use for it.

31

NELLY

Ye never spends on me no more, does ye, Johnny?
Ye dropped me like a hot spud when she took up
with ye. I bet she's been a-tellin' lies on me to wean
ye off. I hear how you're lettin' a petticoat run your
engine,—how your breeches is held up with a apron
string. But I stuck up for ye. Any fool, I says,
could see he was sick a takin' sass. He ain't a idjit,
he knows which side his bread is buttered on. First
he'll get his wad, I says, an' then he'll have his fun.

JOHNNY

That may be an' it mayn't.

NELLY

He'll cut loose from that red headed sack a meal,
I says, onct he gets on his feet.

JOHNNY

Maybe I like 'em fat.

NELLY

Then he won't be so a-scairt to call his soul his own.

32

JOHNNY

They're a-listen' to ye gabbin'.

BARTENDER

Blow the whistle, Mrs. Halcomb,—get thin's started.

MADAM

whistles

Ladees an' gents, ladees an' gents,—we has with us tonight a old favorite, our own Frankie, who will sing for ye by request the numbers ye love most.

CROWD

Moth an' the Flame,—Sweet Bunch a Daisies,— Curse of an Aching Heart.

Frankie sings, "The Curse of an Aching Heart." She sings to Johnny. At the conclusion of the verse she dances.

BARTENDER

Purty, ain't it?

MADAM

Aye, but sad. Give me a small un, Barkeep.

BARTENDER

indicating Frankie

Her a-teamin' up with tripe like him, tripe out a the waller.

MADAM

Easy, Barkeep. Johnny's my son, you know.

BARTENDER

Aye, an' for all that he may be mine, too.

MADAM

Ye needn't remind me.

PIANO PLAYER

Ye oughtta take the Keely cure, Lila.

LILA

It ain't in me. It's too late. I picked daisies too long.

34

PIANO PLAYER
indicating Frankie
It wasn't in her.

LILA
It was somepin outside of her,—love.

PIANO PLAYER
Love.

LILA
They're lovers,—that's where they has it on us.
All join in the ending of the song.

FRANKIE
I was singin' oney for you, Johnny. Was ye listenin'?

JOHNNY
Aye, I heard ye.

FRANKIE
Did ye like how I sung?

JOHNNY

Aye, ye sung good. They oughtta give ye more dough.

FRANKIE

I wasn't singin' for money.

JOHNNY

What for then?

FRANKIE

For you, Johnny.

JOHNNY

Well, they oughtta give ye more dough anyway. Let's have a shot.

FRANKIE

Oney seltzer, Johnny, for me.

JOHNNY

calling

A large un an a seltzer.

36

BARTENDER
Aye.

FRANKIE
Like a beautiful white corpse laid out on lavender, all clean an' lovely, that song is.

JOHNNY
How?

FRANKIE
In a parlor fillt with flowers,—lilacs an' calla lilies. They says how when a virgin dies a rose sprouts outen her heart. Do ye put stock in it?

JOHNNY
Some hand might plant it there.

FRANKIE
I wisht we could love like the flowers does, without toil an' sweat. Sometimes I get a feelin', Johnny,— I get a-scairt. What if somepin should happen to come between us?

JOHNNY

You're allus sittin' on a egg.

FRANKIE

It's nowise impossible. I ain't the first ye've knowed.

JOHNNY

I've chanctes enough if I'd a mind to— Well,— they's allus somepin handy.

FRANKIE

excitedly

Show me the floozy ud—

JOHNNY

Close yer gab. They'll hear ye.

FRANKIE

I'll do right by ye, Johnny. Ye can bank on me. I'll never hedge. Everythin' I'll ever get is yours.

JOHNNY

Quiet down. Ye embarrass me.

38

FRANKIE

Ye'll allus remember what ye vowed to me?

JOHNNY

Aye. Tone down. Hush your jaw.

FRANKIE

We vowed to be true as the stars,—me to you, an' you to me, forever. Do ye mind?

JOHNNY

Aye.

FRANKIE

But do ye swear?

JOHNNY

I've sweared arready.

FRANKIE

Then we're wed we are, clove tighter'n ever we'd be by Scripture. Our oath'll hold eternal.

39

JOHNNY

Aye, like the sea holds water.

A shadow overcasts Frankie and Johnny. The light shines on Nelly Bly.

NELLY

Like airin' her panties,—her showin' off thataway. I think it's positive shameful.

LILA

Ye ain't envious or jealous?

NELLY

Me—a her?

LILA

Not a her, Nelly Bly.

NELLY

Pooh, pooh for you. I wouldn't have *him* nowise. But what does he see in her?

LILA

They's been others.

40

NELLY

Oh, hog yer can.

LILA

You an' yer pickin' an' muck rakin'——

NELLY

You're drunk. I won't pay ye no heed.

LILA

She killt yer chanct with Johnny.

NELLY

I hates her insides.

LILA

You hates her 'cause he loves her.

NELLY

He's oney a-pullin' her leg,—a-gettin' what he can.

LILA

He's stringin' her?

41

NELLY

Until the cash runs out.

LILA

They oughtta wash yer mouth with lye.

NELLY

I could prove it.

LILA

How?

NELLY

By snappin' my fingers an liftin' my skirts.

LILA

They ain't no good in men. They is all vile in their base hearts.

NELLY

Her so high an' haughty,—I've a mind to bring her down.

42

LILA

She so lovin' tender,—him so base an' vile.

NELLY

They's a diamond in my tooth, an' I've gold filled garter snaps. I'm the belle a east St. Louis,—an' I has my way with men.

LILA

Him fillin' the air with lies,—her sighin' it in with love. Oh, give me a drink a rotgut.

Curtain

Scene Two

Frankie and *Johnny are sitting at the table in the barroom. The Bartender stands beside them.*

JOHNNY

Liver pie an' calves' foot jelly, chitt'lin's with sauce Béarnaise, poached cucumbers, raw fry, prunes, soufflé with ginger, a large stein a beer,—an' the lady'll have a egg sandwich.
The bartender exits.
to Frankie
All right now, what we got?

FRANKIE

counting
One flag an' six singles,—an' the rest is silver. Eleven, an' one is twelve, an' one is thirteen,—thirteen fifty.

JOHNNY

Where's the rest? That ain't all.

47

FRANKIE
I was a-scairt to show ye.

JOHNNY
Ye haven't been buying somepin? A-buying some-pin without askin' me?

FRANKIE
Oh, no, Johnny.

JOHNNY
All right then, fork out,—hand over.

FRANKIE
That's all I got. Honest, Johnny.

JOHNNY
You're a-holdin' out on me. Git your hands off. Shell out. Show up.

FRANKIE
There ain't a red cent more,—I hope to die.

48

JOHNNY

Has somebody else his finger in the pot? Are ye playin' two hands?

FRANKIE

Johnny!—ye ain't accusin' me? Ye wouldn't have the heart——

JOHNNY

Aye, I'm accusin' ye point blank. Whatcha been doin' with yer dough? How come yer short? Why ain't ye got more?

FRANKIE

That's all I made.

JOHNNY

Keep jawin'. Where's the jack? Why didn't ye make more?

FRANKIE

It was just a down week, Johnny.

49

JOHNNY

Ye mean nobody made nothin'? I know diffrunt. I
know they did. You're a-tellin' what ain't so.

FRANKIE

Sometimes one makes more an' sometimes the other
makes less. It don't run the same allus. Ye can't
judge. I wasn't never this short afore.

JOHNNY

Hold on, I give ye warnin', I gives ye fair honest
warnin'. I can't go on at this rate,—do ye hear?

FRANKIE

I can't do no more——

JOHNNY

Either ye hustle in the cash, or——
lowering his tone
Well, a man's gotta live.

FRANKIE

What do ye mean, Johnny?

50

JOHNNY
Well, I can't see my way clear to——

FRANKIE
Give me one more chanct, Johnny!

JOHNNY
I give ye chanctes enough arready. Either ye knuckle down——

FRANKIE
Ye wouldn't gimme the gate! Remember what ye sweared!

JOHNNY
That goes so long as you live up to your end of the bargain.

FRANKIE
Ain't I givin' ye every cent I can scrape together, tooth an' toenail?

JOHNNY
Well, it ain't enough.

FRANKIE

Gimme another chanct, Johnny. I'll do better by ye, somehow.

JOHNNY

But I'll be castin' around in the meantime. I dasn't gamble on my future.

FRANKIE

I'll get money for ye someway. Kiss me, Johnny.

JOHNNY

Aye,—when ye've showed me the jack.

FRANKIE

Ye won't have to wait long, Johnny. It'll be sooner'n ye expect, mebbe.

JOHNNY

Ye'll have to hurry.—Hold on! What's that bulge in your stockin'?

FRANKIE

What bulge?

JOHNNY

Hoist up your leg.

FRANKIE

Oh, that little bulge down there. That's oney my hankercheef,—

JOHNNY

Give us a feel.

FRANKIE

I allus keeps my hankercheef down there.

JOHNNY

Turn around. Whatcha afeard of? Put yer knee up.

FRANKIE

Oh, do be careful, Johnny. They'll be seein' ya. It ain't modest.

53

JOHNNY

How come ye get so coy a-sudden? Whatcha got in there?

FRANKIE

Ain't I just been tellin' ye?—Excuse me for a minute, Johnny. I'll come right back. Just a instant, Johnny.

JOHNNY

Stay put. Let's see yer noserag.

FRANKIE

Whatever could ye be wantin' to see my hankercheef for?

JOHNNY

Show up yer noserag or I'll dig it out.

FRANKIE

Leave holt on me, Johnny. Don't,—don't!— Johnny,—Johnny!

Johnny draws a roll of bills from her stocking. Frankie buries her head on the table, weeping.

54

JOHNNY

with rising inflection

Oh ho. Oh hooh. Oh hoooooh. Well, I don't wunner. So it was like I thought. I knew there was somepin ye was up to. I could read the lie in ye.

turning on her savagely

Ye floozy! Ye lyin' parlor floozy!

calmly

But I didn't think ye'd sink so low as this.

FRANKIE

weeping

Ye won't ever believe what I'm a-goin' to tell ye. It was all for you, Johnny. I was a-savin' it up to give ye.

JOHNNY

counting

Fifteen, twenty, twenty-five——

FRANKIE

Don't ye know what day tomorrer is? Our anniversary, Johnny.

JOHNNY

Anniversary a what?

FRANKIE

Of our vow. Don'tcha remember? a year ago tomorrer first we sweared.

JOHNNY

Sweared what? Twenty-five, thirty——

FRANKIE

Sweared to be true to each other. Sweared to be
lovers forever.

JOHNNY

Thirty-seven, thirty-eight, forty.

FRANKIE

I was a-goin' to turn it over to ye in one lump sum
a cash like ye allus wanted.

56

JOHNNY

A-stealin' from me,—I never thought ye'd sink so
low as that.

FRANKIE

It's yours, Johnny, like it was from the start. I
oney been keepin' it for ye, to surprise ye with how
much ye owned.

JOHNNY

Knockin' down, what it was.

FRANKIE

An' for ye to spend on whatever ye like.

JOHNNY

Yer filthy money, stole, dishonorable. I could be
unkind an' tell ye to keep it.

FRANKIE

Ye'll take it, Johnny, or ye'll break my heart.

57

JOHNNY

rising

Aye, I'll take it. For money that ye'd get that way wouldn't never do ye no good. Aye, I'll take it. An' also I can wish ye a fond farewell, now that ye've broke my trust. I can see now ye've been schemin' an' connivin' from the day we first met. Ye didn't fool me. I suspicioned ye all along. Aye,—I'll take what's comin' to me, an' bid ye goodbye,—an' may ye forget as best yer conscience'll allow.

FRANKIE

Ye ain't ditchin' me, Johnny?

JOHNNY

Aye, I'm a-lightin' out for good.

FRANKIE

There won't be none,—none'll do for ye as I've done, Johnny,—give ye their life's blood.

58

JOHNNY

I can oney be thankful I got this to tide me, now
I'm a-strikin' out alone.

FRANKIE

None'll pump their veins dry for ye, Johnny, to
keep ye in clover,—a-doin' that what God an' laws
ferbid, for the sake a love alone.

JOHNNY

You're a-biddin' yourself up too almighty damn
high,—they's dozens.

FRANKIE

Where are they? Look for 'em,—try an' find 'em,
Johnny! Ye won't. Ye won't find them who'll sin
their souls away for love, for you.

JOHNNY

Maybe I know where to look. Maybe they's one,—
one who's been waitin', one in pertikkiler.
He gets up and walks to the door.

FRANKIE

Ye mean—Johnny! Ye dasn't!—or I won't account for what I do. You're my man! Ye dasn't do me wrong!

Curtain

Scene Three

The *street. At left a framesaloon; center, a brick hotel flaunting the motto "Transient." A red light gleams in a second-story window. At right a pawnshop. This was the shop that had "no balls at all." It is a summer evening. Lila staggers into view, waving a bottle.*

61

LILA

K<small>I-YI</small>, ki-yi, I'm fulla alkali. Oh, aint it simply
terrible the way my insides are.
Nelly Bly leans out of the window. Lila sings.
Oh, I don't want to be a drunkard,
An' I'll tell you the reason why,——
My Lord sittin' in his kingdom
Got his eye on me.
The Sheriff enters.
Scat, scat,—get away! I never seen so many. Get
away, do ye hear, or I'll fix ye. They're a-crawlin'
up under my dresses. Scat!—scat! Rats an' snakes!
Save me, save me!

SHERIFF

What's the matter there, little lady?

LILA

They's a whole menagerie a rodents inside my skirts.

SHERIFF

lifting Lila's dresses
How's that?

LILA

They've et my legs away.

SHERIFF

What has? I don't see nothin'.

LILA

Vermin—vermin! Oh, try an' do somepin!

SHERIFF

Aye, we'll fix 'em for ye. Come along with me.

LILA

Ki-yi, whoops! I'm fulla alkali.
They go off.
Johnny comes out of the saloon, the wad of green-backs in his fist.

64

JOHNNY

serenely

There's a load off my chest.

NELLY

Pst! Pst!

Johnny spies her. She beckons.

Ain't he the sight to behold,—like he was bred in a barber shop. I can smell him all the way up here. That juice he's got in his hair that slicks it so lovely.

JOHNNY

pertly

Are ye talkin' to yourself?

NELLY

Who do ye spose I'm talkin' to? Who is it down there is so killin' dressed up in such lovely duds? Where was ye headin' for?

JOHNNY

I was a-goin' callin'.

NELLY

Now ain't that queer?

JOHNNY

Ain't what?

NELLY

Ain't that funny, I says. My nose has been itchin'.
Have ye et your dinner?

JOHNNY

No, I ain't.

NELLY

Hadn't ye better run up an' have a snack? Ye ain't
a-scairt, are ye?

JOHNNY

A-scairt a what?

NELLY

A somebody seein' ye.

66

JOHNNY

Who?

NELLY

Oh, don't go pullin' that. We ain't talkin' in riddles.

JOHNNY

That's all done over with. I ain't a-sneakin' up back stairs no longer.....Get yourself fixed.
He watches Nelly withdraw, then goes to the door and knocks. The Madam opens.
Hello, ma.

MADAM

Howdy, son. Where's Frankie?

JOHNNY

pointing to the saloon
Down there's where I left her. I ain't seen her come out.

MADAM

Good Lord! Whatcha doin' with that big fistful a money in your hand?

JOHNNY

A-keepin' tight holt on it.

MADAM

Wherever did ye get it?

JOHNNY

Outen my bank. I just closed my account.

MADAM

That's the dough as Frankie was a-savin' up to give
ye, ain't it? Lord, oh Lord! Whatever are ye goin'
to do with such a wad?—Ye ain't a-goin' to blow
it in?

JOHNNY

Is it fish outen your fry?

MADAM

If it was you'd never have holt on it. I ain't blind,
Johnny. I could see what's been a-goin' on. It ain't
right.

68

JOHNNY

Right? What ain't?

MADAM

You're a-blowin' in your woman's money.

JOHNNY

Close your box.

MADAM

Squeezin' her like a dishrag.

JOHNNY

It's velvet, ain't it?

MADAM

For you it is. Velvet, did ye say? Aye, velvet,—
velvet for Johnny.
*The Prizefighter comes out of the saloon and
listens, unobserved.*

JOHNNY

If ye wasn't my mother, I'd smack your ears.

69

MADAM

I can see what you're headin' for, but there's no use warnin' ye.

JOHNNY

Get outta my way.

MADAM

Where are ye a-goin'?

JOHNNY

Upstairs. Lemme by.

MADAM

To that lyin' badger bone that'll fleece ye clean. Why don't ye stay in 202 where ye belong?

JOHNNY

I'm a-changin' my quarters.
He pushes his way in.

MADAM

raising her hands
God save him from hisself!

70

She follows him inside.
The Prizefighter goes to the hotel door and listens.
Frankie comes out of the saloon. Her hair is
loosened and her dress is torn at the shoulder.

FRANKIE

I didn't suspect to find the same world here on the
outside. I thought it would all a come to ashes an'
mire, an' it would all be dead save me who was dyin'.
But what I see is a breathin' lovely world, made
lovelier still by a night as was made for lovers.

PRIZEFIGHTER

Was ye a-lookin' for your man?

FRANKIE

Oh,—it's you, Prizefighter.

PRIZEFIGHTER

slyly

Do you want to know where your man's went to?

71

FRANKIE

Johnny?

PRIZEFIGHTER

Aye, Johnny.

FRANKIE

Have ye seed him?

PRIZEFIGHTER

snickering

Aye,—but I spoke afore I meant. I dasn't be tellin'
ye, maybe.

FRANKIE

furiously

What are ye a-holdin' back? Ye stinkin' rat!—
what's up your sleeve? Ye'd best be quick an' work
your jaw, or I'll——

PRIZEFIGHTER

cringing

What's ailin' ye? Let go me. I hasn't done nothin'.
Are ye drunk?

72

FRANKIE

Aye, I'm drunk. Forgive me, Prizefighter. I didn't mean ye no harm. What did ye see?
Johnny and Nelly Bly appear at the window, making love.

PRIZEFIGHTER

I seen your lovingest man. He was a-rowin' with his maw. He was a-goin' upstairs with a wad a greenbacks in his hand, to the parlor on the second floor front.

FRANKIE

seizing him by the throat
Ye liar! I'll dig your eyes outen your head.

PRIZEFIGHTER

struggling in her grasp, he sees the pair at the window
Look! Look!—what I was tellin' ye!
With a low cry, Frankie loosens her hold. The Prizefighter frees himself.
I could a-tolt ye any time he's been a-cheatin'. We

was surprised ye couldn't see it. Like the nose on your face, that plain it was. But no one had the heart to set ye wise. Ye was so dippy on him. Ye ought a run your course different, Frankie. He was a bad un ever for ye to tie to. They was others,— so near ye could spit on 'em,—as would a done different by ye. Not tax ye like he done.

FRANKIE
with sudden wild anger
I'll do for the lot of ye.
then, calmly
Listen, Prizefighter,—ye'd best go off now for a spell. They's business cut out for me.

PRIZEFIGHTER
Ye ain't thinkin' on anythin' rash?

FRANKIE
They's a parcel waitin' for me in the pawnshop there.

74

PRIZEFIGHTER

Come on downstairs with me and take yourself a drink. Ye look wan.

FRANKIE

shouting

Clear out, I'm tellin ye! Don't hinder me none. I'm after my man who's a-doin' me wrong!

She runs into the pawnshop. The Prizefighter follows for a few steps and looks through the pawnshop window. Then shouting, he dashes into the saloon. Frankie reappears immediately with a pistol in her hand. She knocks at the hotel door.

Open up!

There is an instant's silence.

....Open up quick!

She knocks again.

Then stand aside all a ye! Stand back ye floozies, or I'll blow ye all to hell!

She breaks the lock with a shot. The door flies open. She disappears. Nelly Bly and Johnny stare out of the window.

75

JOHNNY

What was that? I heerd a gun shot.
*The Prizefighter, the Bartender and the Piano
Player come from the saloon.*

PRIZEFIGHTER

Under her sky blue kimono she's a big forty-four
gun. They's blood in her eye.
*Another shot is heard, then Nelly's sobbing and
wailing. Johnny appears at the window and goes
to jump out but is pulled back.*

JOHNNY

off stage
Oh, good Lord, Frankie,—don't shoot!—don't
shoot!
suddenly frantic
Help! Help!
then whimpering again
Ye wouldn't kill me, Frankie!
*Johnny backs out the door, followed by Frankie,
whose gun is pressed to his breast.*

76

Ye wouldn't lay me down in cold blood!
*The Madam, coming after Frankie, watches as
though hypnotized with amazed fearful eyes.*
Oh, good Lord, mercy!

FRANKIE

Speak to your Lord and call him good, he's let ye
live so long.

JOHNNY

Ye wouldn't crimp the man who loves ye, Frankie!

FRANKIE

I dasn't stare ye in the eye lest I should weaken.

JOHNNY

Throw aside your gun and kiss me, Frankie.

FRANKIE

Say goodbye to me, Johnny,—say fare thee well.
You're a-travelin' far tonight. You're a-goin' where
the sun'll never find ye. Say goodbye.

JOHNNY

Goodbye.

FRANKIE

Later on I may meet ye, I may see ye over there.
Fare thee well, Johnny.

JOHNNY

Fare thee well.
She fires once. Johnny staggers. She fires again.
Oh, please, Frankie, don't shoot me no more, don't
shoot me no more.
She fires a third time.

MADAM

She's drilled him clean. Ye can see the starlight
through him.
The tune Frankie and Johnny *starts.*

JOHNNY

They lower him to the ground.
Lay me down easy,—roll me over slow. Roll me
on my right side, for the bullet hurt me so.

78

Frankie sobs.

I want to be buried with the clothes I has on me.
Don't ye even unbutton my boots. I want ten crap-
shooters as pallbearers, an' a coal black horse to
carry me off.

When I die just bury me in a box-back coat and
     hat,
Put a twenty-dollar gold piece in my mouth
So the Lord'll know I'm standin' pat.
Frankie, Frankie, oh my baby, kiss me onct, just
     onct afore I go.—Who *was* your man,—who
     done you wrong.

*The music swells, the bass is profound, while
Frankie kisses Johnny.*

FRANKIE

What's that a-rumblin' away down in the ground?

MADAM

It's my little baby Johnny goin down,—down,—
down.

79

FRANKIE

There ain't no time to lose,—I got to be jinin' him.
Go after the Sheriff. Get the law.

MADAM

It's not murder in the second degree——

BARTENDER

It's not murder in the third——

FRANKIE

I simply dropped my man, as a hunter drops his
bird.

*The ten macks dance in bearing a coffin. The
music is recitative. They tap out the time as they
lower Johnny into the box and carry him off. The
others follow, singing,—*

> *Eleven men goin' to the graveyard*
> *All in a rubber-tired hack.*

Eleven men goin' to the graveyard
Oney ten comin' back....
He was her man,
But he done....

Curtain

Epilogue

*A*t the scaffold, as in the prologue.

FRANKIE

WIPE the water from your eye, Sheriff. It may hinder ye in your job. We mustn't welch now, we got somepin to do together,—not thinkin' on ourselves, but on what it'll come to. Without it endin' thisaway, they'd be no point to the story.

SHERIFF

But I wash *my* hands clean.

FRANKIE

What time is it gettin'?

SHERIFF

It's gettin' *the* time, Frankie,—*the* time.

FRANKIE

I felt the seconds flyin' faster by.

SHERIFF

Whoever'll take leave of the condemned had best speak out.

CROWD

Farewell, Frankie, farewell.

MADAM

I can't forgive ye, Frankie,—I dasn't, for blood's thicker'n water. But I wish ye a soft berth wherever you're goin'. An' the bed in 202'll be kept fresh an' empty, so Johnny an' you won't be castin' around for a place to lay easy when ye make your honeymoon.

FRANKIE

We'll pay ye a visit, Mrs. Halcomb, like respectable married folk.

LILA

Goodbye, Frankie. I wishes ye a speedy journey, an' I'll leave a bottle out under the moon tonight for ye to sip from as ye passes. I'll think on ye allus.

FRANKIE

So long, Bartender.

BARTENDER

We'll draw a large un for ye, an' fix ye a snack, an set it down to your place as if ye was by us. We'll toast to ye, Frankie, like we allus done.

FRANKIE

Thankee, Bartender, no prayer could be more fitten.

PIANO PLAYER

An' we'll strike up a chune for ye, Frankie, for your sperit to dance by.

87

FRANKIE

Ye'd best start your tune up now, Dopey,—I'll be dancin' for ye in a minute.

PIANO PLAYER

An' none for your partner. This time ye dance alone.

FRANKIE

Ye can all be my partners.

SHERIFF

All right, Frankie,—are ye ready? Let's make short work of it so long as it has got to be.
The music starts, Frankie and Johnny *in lively ragtime.*

FRANKIE

The way I'd like to go out,—you a-dancin' down there, me a-dancin' up here. Would that be suiten to ye?

88

LILA

Aye, we'll dance with ye, Frankie. We'll tread your measure.

FRANKIE

Ye'll have to dance lively. I'll be showin' ye new steps in a minute, steps ye've never seen afore.

MADAM

We'll follow ye, Frankie, we'll learn the steps from ye.

FRANKIE

Give me the sign when ye're ready, Sheriff.

SHERIFF

Three's the word.

FRANKIE

to the crowd
Unlimber your legs! Get thin's started!

SHERIFF
marking time with his hand
One——

CROWD
Farewell, Frankie, farewell.

SHERIFF
Two——

FRANKIE
Clap your hands. Keep to my time. Let's see ye
dance.

SHERIFF
Three.
*The rope sings then snaps like a larrup. The crowd
turn away their heads. There is a long cry. The
Sheriff falls to his knees. Suddenly he rises.*
Let's show her ghost we're a-keepin' our trust.
Dance, all of ye.

CROWD
Dance,—dance!
90

SHERIFF

Dance till ye keel over,—dance the chill away!

CROWD

Dance!

SHERIFF

We dasn't let her cold get into our bones. We got to keep dancin'.

CROWD

Dancin'——

The ten macks dance in, single file.

Curtain

Frankie and Albert

THE ST. LOUIS VERSION

FRANKIE AND ALBERT

FRANKIE and Albert were lovers, O Lordy, how
    they could love.
Swore to be true to each other, true as the stars
    above;
He was her man, but he done her wrong.

Frankie she was a good woman, just like every one
    knows.
She spent a hundred dollars for a suit of Albert's
    clothes.
He was her man, but he done her wrong.

Frankie and Albert went walking, Albert in a
    brand new suit.
"Oh, good Lord," says Frankie, "but don't my Al-
    bert look cute?"
He was her man but he done her wrong.

Frankie went down to Memphis, she went on the evening train.

She paid one hundred dollars for Albert a watch and chain.

He was her man, but he done her wrong.

Frankie lived in the crib house, crib house had only two doors;

Gave all her money to Albert, he spent it on those call house whores.

He was her man, but he done her wrong.

Albert's mother told him, and she was mighty wise,

"Don't spend Frankie's money on that parlor Alice Pry.

You're Frankie's man, and you're doing her wrong."

Frankie and Albert were lovers, they had a quarrel one day,

Albert he up and told Frankie, "Bye-bye, babe, I'm going away.

I was your man, but I'm just gone."

96

Frankie went down to the corner to buy a glass of
beer.
Says to the fat bartender, "Has my lovingest man
been here?
He was my man, but he's doing me wrong."

"Ain't going to tell you no story, ain't going to tell
you no lie,
I seen your man 'bout an hour ago with a girl
named Alice Pry.
If he's your man, he's doing you wrong."

Frankie went down to the pawnshop, she didn't go
there for fun;
She hocked all of her jewelry, bought a pearl-
handled forty-four gun
For to get her man who was doing her wrong.

Frankie she went down Broadway, with her gun in
her hand,
Sayin', "Stand back, all you livin' women, I'm
a-looking for my gambolin' man.
For he's my man, won't treat me right."

Frankie went down to the hotel, looked in the window so high,
There she saw her loving Albert a-loving up Alice Pry.
Damn his soul, he was mining in coal.

Frankie went down to the hotel, she rang that hotel bell.
"Stand back, all of you chippies, or I'll blow you all to hell.
I want my man, who's doing me wrong."

Frankie threw back her kimono, she took out her forty-four,
Root-a-toot-toot three times she shot right through that hotel door.
She was after her man who was doing her wrong.

Albert grabbed off his Stetson, "Oh, good Lord, Frankie, don't shoot!"
But Frankie pulled the trigger and the gun went root-a-toot-toot.
He was her man, but she shot him down.

98

Albert he mounted the staircase, crying, "Oh,
    Frankie, don't you shoot!"
Three times she pulled that forty-four a-root-a-
    toot-toot-toot-toot.
She shot her man who threw her down.

First time she shot him he staggered, second time
    she shot him he fell,
Third time she shot him, O Lordy, there was a new
    man's face in hell.
She killed her man who had done her wrong.

"Roll me over easy, roll me over slow,
Roll me over on my left side for the bullet hurt
    me so.
I was her man, but I done her wrong."

"Oh my baby, kiss me, once before I go.
Turn me over on my right side, the bullet hurt
    me so.
I was your man, but I done you wrong."

Albert he was a gambler, he gambled for the gain,
The very last words that Albert said were, "High-
low Jack and the game."
He was her man but he done her wrong.

Frankie heard a rumbling away down in the
ground.
Maybe it was Albert where she had shot him down.
He was her man and she done him wrong.

Bring out your long black coffin, bring out your
funeral clothes,
Bring out Albert's mother, to the churchyard Albert goes.
He was her man but he done her wrong.

Oh, bring on your rubber-tired hearses, bring on
your rubber-tired hacks,
They're taking Albert to the cemetery and they
ain't a-bringing him back.
He was her man, but he done her wrong.

Eleven macks a-riding to the graveyard, all in a
rubber-tired hack,
Eleven macks a-riding to the graveyard, only ten
a-coming back.
He was her man, but he done her wrong.

Frankie went to the coffin, she looked down on
Albert's face,
She said, "Oh, Lord, have mercy on me, I wish I
could take his place.
He was my man and I done him wrong."

Frankie went to Mrs. Halcomb, she fell down on
her knees,
She said to Mrs. Halcomb, "Forgive me if you
please.
I've killed my man for doing me wrong."

"Forgive you, Frankie darling, forgive you I never
can.
Forgive you, Frankie darling, for killing your only
man.
He was your man, though he done you wrong."

The judge said to the jury, "It's as plain as plain can be.
This woman shot her man, it's murder in the second degree.
He was her man, though he done her wrong."

Now it was not murder in the second degree, it was not murder in the third.
The woman simply dropped her man, like a hunter drops his bird.
He was her man and he done her wrong.

"Oh, bring a thousand policemen, bring them around today,
Oh, lock me in that dungeon and throw the key away.
I killed my man 'cause he done me wrong."

"Oh, put me in that dungeon. Oh, put me in that cell,
Put me where the northeast wind blows from the southwest corner of hell.
I shot my man 'cause he done me wrong."

102

Frankie walked up the scaffold, as calm as a girl
    can be,
And turning her eyes to heaven she said, "Good
    Lord, I'm coming to thee.
He was my man, and I done him wrong."

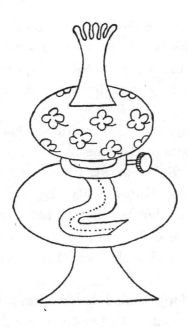

ON THE ST. LOUIS VERSION

In the oldest versions of the song, the name of Frankie's man is Albert. *Frankie and Albert* hails from St. Louis, where a colored sporting woman, and her gambling man, lived out the legend thirty years ago.

"You say, boy, of Frankie she had dice in one hand and a gun in the other."

Frankie Baker of St. Louis, and the sporting circuit, Omaha, Kansas City, Denver, San Francisco, Chicago, shot her man in her twenty-seventh year, having already gained notoriety by her open handedness, good looks, and her proud and racy bearing.

"For a long time I knew Frankie quite well and kept in touch with her for a number of years

104

but lately (since marrying) have lost track of her although think she is in Portland. . . . I have talked with Frankie on different times concerning this shooting and never thought of asking her just why of the killing as it seemed to annoy her.

"She was a beautiful, light brown girl, who liked to make money and spend it. She dressed very richly, sat for company in magenta lady's cloth, diamonds as big as hen's eggs in her ears. There was a long razor scar down the side of her face she got in her teens from a girl who was jealous of her. She only weighed about a hundred and fifteen pounds, but she had the eye of one you couldn't monkey with. She was a queen sport."

She was a queen sport in a society which for flamboyant elegance and fast living ranks alone in the sporting west.

This society was built around the woman and her mack. It began in the period of restoration with the river men bringing girls to the levees and the railroad camps to fill the work gang's need for women.

New Orleans had already had her *maquereau,* a colored exquisite, who made his percentage out of the sporting white's weakness for black girls. But the maquereau was a hanger-on. His girls could get along without him. The river man was of a different stripe. He parlayed what his woman turned over, in games with the work hands. He was a card sharp, a finished gambler.

When their pockets were full of spikes, the pair would turn their faces to a live town. St. Louis was filling in with their like. Before long it was a sporting depot, with tracks running east to Chicago and west towards the coast. Macking had become a full-fledged business. The smartest macks touted the women who could take in the most, then gambled between themselves. The play was always for high stakes and a great deal of money changed hands.

St. Louis became known as the toughest town in the west. Boogie-joints and bucket-shops opened up on Twelfth, Carr, Targee, and Pine Streets. The fast colored men and women lived up to their necks. Stack-o-lee stepped out and made a legend of his Stetson hat. The girls wore red for Billy Lyons. Duncan killed Brady. The ten pimps that bore the dead were kept on parade between the infirmary and the graveyard.

The advent of the mack was something new in the American scene. His dress and his gamey affectations quickened the tempo of the life around him.

He invented styles that took the eye of the sporting world at large.......The St. Louis flats, heel-less, and of extra length for the men off the steamboats who had gone barefoot so long they could not stand the cramp of regular shoes. Mirrors were set in the toes. Gaiters matched the velvet trouser cuff, the vest, and hat,—the Stetson high roller, with nudes and racers inlaid with eyelets in the crown. The linens were of fine quality, with starched, embroidered bosoms and cuffs,—the cuffs worn low so that the diamond solitaire on the little finger just showed.......And the wealth of jewelry, solvent diamonds,—diamond suspender clasps, sleeve garters, diamond initials on the watch ribbon, diamonds in the teeth.

> "Put a twenty-dollar gold piece on my watch chain
> To let the Lord know I'm standing pat."

The gold piece was the note of humility. No matter how high a man's fortune, he always wore his gold piece. So long as he had it he was not broke. At the tail-end of his luck the gold piece was always the last to go.

FRANKIE shot Allen Britt on October 15, 1899. Allen, or Albert, as he liked to be called, was a tall, slender, ginger boy, only seventeen years old. He first met Frankie at a ball in Stoles hall, at 13th and Biddle streets. Soon afterwards he went to live with her at 212 Targee street, where Frankie sat for company.

Richard Clay, a St. Louis negro, knew Albert very well. He was with him at the ball the night he met Frankie, and he talked with Albert when the boy was dying at the City Hospital..........

"Frankie loved Albert all right. He was wise for his years but not old enough to be level with any woman. Frankie was ready money. She bought him everything he wanted, and kept his pockets full. Then while she was waiting on company he would be out playing around."

On the Sunday night of the shooting Frankie went out to look for Albert. She surprised him in the hallway of the old Phoenix hotel, making up to a girl named Alice Pryar.[1] She called Albert outside and began quarreling with him. A crowd gathered and listened to the row. Albert would not go home with her. Finally she went on alone. It was nearly daylight when Albert followed. He found Frankie waiting up for him. There was more quarreling as he got ready for bed. He admitted to Frankie that he had been with Alice in her room at the hotel, and he warned her that he was ready to throw her over for good. She began to cry and said she was going to find Alice Pryar. Albert said he would kill her if she tried to go. She started for the door and Albert threw the lamp at her. In the darkness Frankie shot him as he came after her with a knife.

Albert made his way out of the house and down the street to the home of his parents at number 32. His mother heard him calling. She came out and found him lying on the front steps in his pajamas. He told her what had happened, and she began to scream, "Frankie's shot Allen! Frankie's shot Allen!"

. . . ."Inside of a few minutes the word was all over that Frankie had gotten her man."

Albert was taken to the City Hospital. He died at 2:15 on the morning of the 19th with a bullet wound of the liver.[2]

Frankie gave herself up at the Four Courts. She was released after the inquest on the coroner's decision of justifiable homicide.

Allen Britt, son of George and Nancy Britt, was buried in St. Peter's cemetery, October 22, 1899.[3]

On the 19th of October the St. Louis *Post-Despatch* ran this account of the story:

AMID THE SUFFERING

"Allen Britt's brief experience in the art of love cost him his life. He died at the City Hospital Wednesday night from knife wounds inflicted by Frankie Baker, an ebony hued cake-walker. Britt was also colored. He was seventeen years old. He met Frankie at the Orange Blossom's ball and was smitten with her. Thereafter they were lovers.

"In the rear of 212 Targee street lived Britt. There his sweetheart wended her way a few nights ago and lectured Allen for his alleged duplicity. Allen's reply was not intended to cheer the dusky damsel and a glint of steel gleamed in the darkness. An instant later the boy fell to the floor mortally wounded.

"Frankie Baker is locked up at the Four Courts."

FRANKIE BAKER is still alive. She lives in Portland, Oregon, where she runs a shoe shining parlor. She is fifty-eight years old. The song has not been traced to any Frankie before her.

NOTES

(1) Alice Pryar, eighteen years. No permanent home. Prostitute.

(2) City Hospital Record.

> Frankie Baker shot Allen Britt on the night of October 15, 1899. He died at 2:15 A M on the 19th day of October with a bullet wound of the liver. He lived seventeen years in the city before his death. He was born in Kentucky, and lived at 212 Targee street. His occupation at the time of entering the hospital given as job worker.

(3) Nancy Britt is still living at 32 Johnson (formerly Targee) street, St. Louis.

Frankie and Albert
THE OTHER VERSIONS

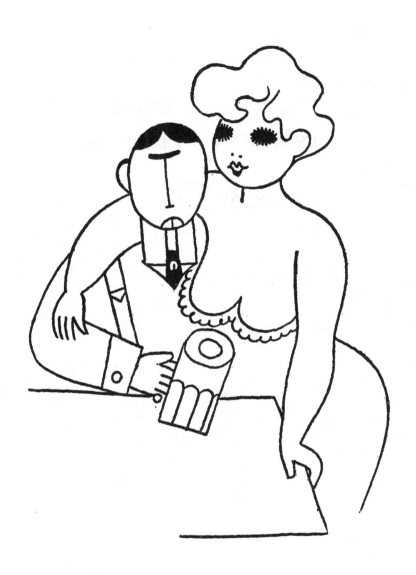

FRANCES SHE SHOT ALBERT

From Prof. H. M. Belden
WEST VIRGINIA

CHORUS:

He's her man but he done-a her wrong.
He's her man but he done-a her wrong.

FRANCES was a good girl,
She always went to school.
The only fault that Frances had
Was that she was a fool.

Albert was a bad man,
He always liked to sin.
The only fault that Albert had
Was drinking too much gin.

Albert was a bad boy,
He never did do right.
The only thing that Albert did
Was gamble, drink and fight.

Frances was so gentle;
She always liked to cook.
The boys they didn't like her much,
For she had that Romy look.

Frances she met Albert,
'Twas at a shooting match.
She smiled at Albert sweetly,
His eye she tried to catch.

He looked at Frankie once,
He looked at Frankie twice.
The third time he looked at Frankie
Says, "She looks passing nice."

He saw her in the church one night,
He'd peeked in through the door.
But when he saw a man with her,
He walked away and swore.

Albert he kissed Frankie
Outside her mother's gate.
"Oh, please don't do that, Albert,
I'd have you know I'm straight."

Albert he hugged Frankie
As they were walkin' slow.
"Please don't do that, Albert,
For 'twill make my honor go."

Then right at once poor Frankie
To her little mother ran.
"Mother, I love Albert
I want him for my man."

That mother she did know best,
As only mothers can.
Pleaded with her daughter
Never to marry a gambling man.

"Listen, oh my daughter,
To little mother dear.
Please don't marry Albert,
For he's a gamble-eer."

The wedding took place early,
At early candle light;
'Twas in her mother's cabin,
That little house so tight.

They found a parson sleeping,
They found him taking rest.
They made that parson get up
And marry them undressed.

The parson was an old man,
His hair was awful white,
His beard it covered all his chest
When he married them that night.

Frankie she shot Albert,
And I'll tell you the reason why,
Ever' dollar bill she gave Albert,
He'd give it to Alice Blye.

She went down Fourth street
With a long knife in her hand,
Says, "Stand aside, you drunks and bums,
I'm lookin' for my man."

She went into a hop joint,
And she didn't go for fun.
For under her apron
She carried a forty-four gun.

She went into a hop joint,
And ordered a bottle of beer.
Says to the bartender,
"Have you seen my Albert here?"

"Now don't tell me no story,
Now don't tell me no lie;
If Albert's got that girl in here,
He's shorely got to die."

"I won't tell you no story,
I won't tell you no lie;
Albert left here a little while ago
With little Alice Blye."

"Looka here, now, Albert,
I'm fearin' for my life.
That woman standin' in the door
She is your gentle wife."

Frankie shot at Albert once,
She shot at Albert twice;
Third time she shot at Albert
She took poor Albert's life.

They took him to a hospital,
His life they tried to save;
But they didn't do him any good,
For now he's in his grave.

"Turn me over, Frankie,
Turn me over slow,
Because them leaden bullets
They did hurt me so."

"No! I can't forgive you, Frankie,
No! woman, I never can.
He was your only husband,
Though he was a naughty man."

For miles around came people,
Yes, to that funeral came.
They kept their faces covered,
So no one knew their name.

121

They took him to that cemetery
In a rubber-tired hack,
They took him to that cemetery
But they did not bring him back.

The judge says to the jury,
"Now listen here to me,
This woman shot her husband
But I'm goin' to set her free."

AMY AND ALBERT

From Frederick S. Henry, the Tome School,
Port Deposit, MARYLAND

Amy was a good woman,
Everybody knows,
She spent ten thousand dollars
To buy her Albert clothes.

CHORUS: *He was her man, but he done her wrong.*

Amy went to the corner
To buy a pint of beer;
Says Amy to the barkeep,
"Is my Albert here?"

Barkeep says to Amy,
"Ain't goin' to tell no lies;

Your Albert's up in the back room
With a girl called Alco Lize."

Amy went up the back stairs,
She didn't go for fun.
Beneath her gingham apron
She carried a double-barreled gun.

She pulled aside that curtain,
She pulled the trigger twice;
The second time she pulled it
She took her Albert's life.

Rubber-tired buggy,
Rubber-tired hack,
They took poor Albert to the cemetery,
But they didn't bring him back.

Amy says to the warden,
"What will the sentence be?"
The warden says to Amy,
"It's th' electric chair for thee."

125

Put poor Amy in th' electric chair,
Turned the current on;
Ten thousand volts through Amy;
I wonder where she's gone.

FRANKIE

Alice Childs in MOUNTAIN WHITES, 1928

Frankie was a good girl as everybody knowed
She paid forty dollars for Johnny a suit of clothes,
But he done her wrong, he done her wrong.

Frankie went out walking, she walked upon the
main;
She paid twenty dollars for Johnny a watch and
chain;
But he done her wrong, he done her wrong.

Frankie went to the bartender's and called for a
glass of beer.
She says to the bartender, "Has Johnny Gray been
here?
He's done me wrong, he's done me wrong."

The bartender says to Frankie, "I won't tell you
no lie,
He passed here an hour ago with a girl named
Nelsie Fly.
He's done you wrong, he's done you wrong."

Frankie went out walking, she didn't walk for fun,
She placed on her apron and smokeless forty-one,
To kill her man, for he done her wrong.

The first time she shot he fell down on his knees,
He says to the policeman, "Don't let her kill me,
please.
For I done her wrong, I done her wrong."

Frankie went to her mother's, she fell down on her
bed,
She says to her mother, "I killed poor Johnny dead,
But he done me wrong, he done me wrong."

In came Frankie's father, and says, "What makes
you sigh?

For every nickel and dime he gets he spends on
  Nelsie Fly.
He done you wrong, he done you wrong."

In came Frankie's sister, and says, "What makes
  you weep?
If Johnny Gray had been a man of mine, I'd a-
  killed him away last week!
He's done you wrong, he's done you wrong."

Frankie went to the graveyard, she fell down on
  her knees,
She says to her Johnny, "Speak to me a word of
  ease.
For I've done you wrong, I've done you wrong."

FRANKIE BAKER

From AMERICAN MOUNTAIN SONGS
compiled by Ethel Park Richardson

LITTLE Frankie went down to the barroom
She called for a glass of beer.
She asked the barkeeper
"Has my lovin' Albert been here?
He's my man, won't treat me right."

The barroom keeper says, "Frankie,
I'm tellin' you no lie
He left here just a minute ago
With a gal called Alice Fry.
If he's your man, won't treat you right."

131

Little Frankie went down Broadway
With a razor in her hand,
Sayin', "Stand back, all you livin' women,
I'm a-lookin' for my gambolin' man,
For he's my man, won't treat me right."

Little Albert run round the table,
An' he fell down on his knees,
Cryin' out, "Frankie, don't shoot me,
Don't shoot me,—if you please!
For I'm your man, goin' treat you right."

It was on a Friday morning,
'Bout half past nine o'clock.
Frankie grabbed her forty-four gun
An' fired two fatal shots,
Killed the man wouldn't treat her right.

"Please turn me over, Frankie,
Please turn me over slow,
But do not touch my wounded side,
Or my heart will overflow.
You've killed him dead wouldn't treat you right."

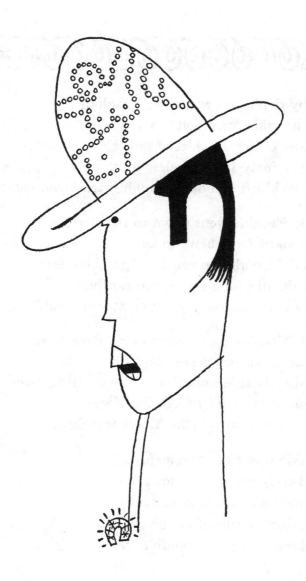

"Why don't you run now, Frankie?
Oh, Frankie, why don't you run?
Yonder comes the chief of police
With a forty-fo' smokeless gun.
You've killed him dead wouldn't treat you right."

Little Frankie went down to the river,
She looked from bank to bank,
Sayin', "Do all you can for a gamblin' man,
And then he won't give you no thank,
For a gamblin' man won't treat you right."

Little Frankie then looked down Broadway
As far as she could see.
Couldn't hear nothin' but a three-string band
Playin' *Nearer, My God, To Thee.*
All over the town little Albert was dead!

Frankie was a good woman,
As shorely everyone knows.
She paid a hundred dollar bill
For Albert a suit of clothes.
She loved the man wouldn't treat her right.

Little Frankie is now in prison
With her back turned to the wall.
She is writin' letters to the boys and girls
Sayin' gamblin' was the cause of it all.
For a gamblin' man won't treat you right.

They took little Frankie to the courthouse,
They put her in a big arm chair.
Then the judge an' the jury said,
"I'll give you ninety-nine years free
For shootin' the man wouldn't treat you right."

LILLY

Version of Harold W. Odum,
in Journal of AMERICAN FOLK LORE,
December, 1911

LILLY was a good girl, everybody knows.
Spent a hundred dollars to buy her father's suit of
  clothes.
Her man certainly got to treat her right.

She went to Bell street—bought a bottle of beer;
"Good morning, bar-keeper, has my lovin' man
  been here?
My man certainly got to treat me right."

"It is Sunday and I ain't goin' to tell you no lie,
He was standin' over there just an hour ago.
Your man certainly got to treat you right."

She went down to First avenue to pawnbroker.
"Good morning, kind lady, what will you have?"
"I want to get a forty-four gun, for
All I got's done gone."

He said to the lady, "It's against my law
To rent any woman forty-four smokin' gun,
For all you got'll be dead and gone."

She went to the alley—dogs begin to bark,—
Saw her lovin' man standin' in the dark,
Laid his poor body down.

"Turn me over, Lilly, turn me over slow,
May be las' time, I don't know,
All you got's dead and gone."

She sent for the doctors—doctors all did come;
Sometimes they walk, sometimes they run,
An' it's one more rounder gone.

They picked up Pauly, carried him to infirmary,
He told the doctor he's a gambling man.
An' it's one more rounder gone.

138

Newsboys come runnin' to tell th' mother th' news.
She said to the lads, "That can't be true,
I seed my son 'bout an hour ago."

"Come here, John, and get your hat,
Go down the street, an' see where my son is at,
Is he gone? Is he gone?"

The policemen all dressed in blue,
They come down the street by two an' two,
One mo' rounder gone.

"Lucy git your bonnet. Johnny git your hat.
Go down on Bell street, an' see where my son is at.
Is he gone? Is he gone?"

Sunday she got 'rested, Tuesday she was fined,
Wednesday she pleaded for all life trial,
An' it's all she's got's done gone.

She said to the jailer, "How can I sleep?
All roun' my bedside lovin' Paul do creep.
It's all I got's gone."

The wimmins in Atlanta, they hear the news,
Run excursions with new red shoes,
An' it's one more rounder gone.

Well, they pick up Pauly an' laid him to rest.
Preacher said the ceremony, sayin':
"Well, it's all that you've got's dead an' gone."

FRANKY

Version of F. R. Rubel,
in Journal of AMERICAN FOLK LORE

FRANKY went down the bayou;
Franky heard a bull dog bark;
Franky said, "That's Johnny
Hiding in the dark.
For he's my man; but he's done me wrong."

Franky went down a dark alley;
Heard a bull dog bark:
And there lay her Johnny
Shot right through the heart.
"Oh, he's my man; but he's done me wrong."

Franky went on the witness stand;
The judge says, "Don't tell no lie.
When did you shoot poor Johnny?
Did you intend for him to die?
Oh, he's your man; but he's done you wrong."

Oh, rubber-tired buggy,
Rubber-tired hack,
Took poor Johnny to the cemetery,
But it never brought him back.
"Oh, he's my man; but he's dead an' gone."

ALBERT

Version of Glen H. Mullin,
in ADVENTURES OF A SCHOLAR TRAMP

Albert was a bad man.....as everybody knows.
Albert was a rounder.....but he certainly wore
good clothes.
Oh, he's my man.....but he done me wrong.

Some folks gives Albert a nickel, and some gives
Albert a dime,
But I don't give Albert a frazzlin' cent, kase he
ain't no fren' o' mine,

Oh, he's my man, but he done me wrong.

Oh, I went down to that hop-joint, an' I rung the
hop-joint bell,

145

An' there sat Albert a-hittin' the pipe, a-hittin' the
    pipe to beat hell.

Oh, he's my man, but he done me wrong.

Turn me over, doctor, turn me over slow;
She said she shot me with a thirty-eight, but I know
    'twas a forty-fo'.

Oh, I'm her man, but I done her wrong.

FRANKIE AND ALBERT

Version of Roberta Anderson, TEXAS
Published in ON THE TRAIL OF NEGRO FOLK SONGS,
by Dorothy Scarborough

FRANKIE was a good woman,
As everybody knows.
She bought her po' Albert
A bran' new suit o' clos'
Oh, he's her man,
But he done her wrong!

Barkeeper said to Frankie,
"I won't tell you no lies;
I saw yo' po' Albert
Along with Sara Slies.

147

Oh, he's yo' man,
But he done yo' wrong!"

An' then they put po' Albert
In a bran' new livery hack
Took him to the graveyard,
But they never brought him back.
Oh, he's her man,
But he done her wrong!

FRANKIE AND ALBERT

Version of Louise Garwood, Houston, TEXAS.
Published in
ON THE TRAIL OF NEGRO FOLK SONGS
by Dorothy Scarborough

FRANKIE was a good woman,
Everybody knows.
Paid about a hundred dollars
For the making of Albert's clothes—
    "Oh, he was my man,
        But he done me wrong!"

Standing on the street corner,
Didn't mean no harm.
Up in the second-story window
Saw Alice in Albert's arms!
    "Oh, he was my man,
        But he done me wrong!"

149

Frankie went down to the saloon,
Didn't go there for fun;
Underneath her silk petticoat
She carried a forty-one gun.
    "Oh, he was my man,
        But he done me wrong!"

"Listen here, Mr. Bartender,
  Don't you tell me no lies.
  Have you seen that Nigger Albert
  With the girl they call the Katy Fly?
    Oh, he was my man,
        But he done me wrong."

Frankie shot Albert once,
Frankie shot Albert twice,
Third time she shot poor Albert
She took that Nigger's life.
    "Oh, he was my man,
        But he done me wrong!"

Rubber-tired carriages
Kansas City hack,

Took poor Albert to the cemetery,
But forgot to bring him back.
"Oh, he was my man,
But he done me wrong!"

FRANKIE AND ALBERT

*Version of W. H. Thomas, Professor of English
at Agricultural and Mechanical College of Texas;
former President of Texas Folk Lore Society*

FRANKIE went to the bar-keeper's to get a bottle
    of beer;
She says to the bar-keeper: "Has my lovin' babe
    been here?"
He was her man, babe, but he done her wrong.

The bar-keeper says to Frankie: "I ain't goin' to
    tell you no lie
Albert passed long here walkin' about an hour ago
    with a nigger named Alkali."
He was her man, babe, but he done her wrong.

153

Frankie went to Albert's house; she didn't go for
    fun;
For underneath her apron was a blue barrel forty-
    one.
He was her man, babe, but he done her wrong.

When Frankie got to Albert's house, she didn't say
    no word,
But she cut down upon poor Albert just like he was
    a bird.
He was her man, babe, but she shot him down.

When Frankie left Albert's house, she lit out in a
    run,
For underneath her apron was a smoking forty-one.
He was her man, babe, but she shot him down.

"Roll me over, doctor, roll me over slow,
Cause when you roll me over, them bullets hurt
    me so.
I was her man, babe, but she shot me down."

Frankie went to the church house, and fell upon
    her knees,
Cryin': "Oh, Lord, have mercy, won't you give my
    heart some ease?
He was my man, babe, but I shot him down."

Rubber-tired buggy, decorated hack,
They took him to the graveyard, but they couldn't
    bring him back.
He was her man, babe, but he done her wrong.

FRANKIE AND ALBERT

Version of Mrs. Tom Bartlett,
MARLIN, TEXAS. *Published in*
ON THE TRAIL OF NEGRO FOLK SONGS

Frankie was a good woman
Everybody knows.
She paid one hundred dollars
For Albert a suit of clothes!
For he was her man, but he done her wrong.

Frankie went to Albert's house
And found little Alice there!
Pulled out her forty-five
And brought him to the floor!
"He was my man, but he done me wrong!"

157

Frankie went to the court house;
Court house look so high!
Put her foot on the bottom step,
And hung her head and cry,
"Oh, he was my man, but he done me wrong!"

Frankie had two children
A boy and a girl;
Never see their papa any more
Till they meet him in another world.
"Oh, he was my man, but he done me wrong!"

AMY AND ALBERT

Reported from Durham, N. C.
MS. of Blake B. Harrison. (*Expurgated*)
From AMERICAN NEGRO FOLK SONGS
by Newman I. White

AMY was a good woman, everybody knows.
She spent ten thousand dollars to buy her Albert
clothes.
He was her man, but he done her wrong.

Amy went to the bar-room to get a bottle of beer.
Amy says to the bar-tender, "You seen my Albert
here?
He was my man, but he done me wrong."

Bar-tender says to Amy: "I ain't gwine tell you no lies,
I seen your Albert down here wid a woman what had blue eyes,—"
He was her man, but he done her wrong.